# Harry's Ne

Story by Carmel Reilly

Illustrations by Liz Alger

**Rigby**®

A Harcourt Achieve Imprint

www.Rigby.com

1-800-531-5015

Dad got Harry a new hat for school.

"I like this blue and yellow hat," said Harry.

He went off to school with his new hat on.

Harry came home after school without his hat.

"Where is your new hat?" said Dad.

"Oh!" said Harry. "My hat!
I had it on at the playground.
I will have to go back
and get it now."

"I will come with you," said Dad.

Dad and Harry looked for the hat on the school playground.

"I can't see it here at all," said Dad.

"I have lost my new hat," said Harry.

"Come on," said Dad.

"Your hat is not here.

Let's go home."

At home Harry said,
"Dad, I have not looked for my hat
in my school bag."

He opened his bag
and looked inside.

Harry took some books
out of his bag.
Next he got his lunch box out.

Then he saw his new hat.

"Look, Dad!" said Harry with a laugh.

"I have not lost my new hat after all."